MORE Bedtime Stories
TO READ ALOUD

by BARBEE OLIVER CARLETON

Illustrated by CROSBY NEWELL

ACKNOWLEDGMENT

With the exception of "Three Boys in a Tree," which appeared in *Story-a-Day* magazine, all of the stories in this collection first appeared in *Highlights for Children* magazine, and are reprinted by permission of Highlights for Children, Inc., Columbus, Ohio.

© 1951, 1952, 1953, 1954, 1955, 1956, 1957, 1958, 1959, 1960, Highlights for Children, Inc.

CONTENTS

INTRODUCTION

As soon as we began printing stories by Barbee Oliver Carleton in *Highlights for Children*, there came a flood of enthusiasm from children, parents and teachers.

Children from 3 to 6 wanted to hear them read over and over; parents and older children enjoyed reading them.

Each story has a plot and strong suspense. The listener or reader easily identifies himself, in his imagination, with the leading characters. How full of music, imagery and human warmth each story is that comes from Barbee Oliver Carleton!

Garry Cleveland Myers
Editor, *Highlights for Children*

THE TALE OF NAPOLEON MOUSE

IT RAINED and it rained and it rained. And still it kept on raining. Napoleon Mouse sat by the window, cleaning out the cake bowl.

"Any other day," whispered he to himself, "let it rain, and see if I care. But not on Grandma's birthday. Not on the day Grandma Mouse is coming for dinner, even if she does wear her rubbers. Even if she does say, in her cheery way, 'A little rain never hurt anybody.'"

A little rain, indeed!

Napoleon pressed his small black nose

against the pane, and his small black eyes grew rounder and rounder. For the puddle by the gate was no longer just a puddle. It was a little lake, deeper than rubbers, deeper than boots, deeper than Grandma herself!

Back in the kitchen, Mother and Father Mouse and Napoleon's sixteen sisters were ever so busy and gay—much too busy and gay to stare out of windows. With the cake to decorate, they told each other, and the ice cream to freeze, and the little gifts to wrap— with all these things to do before Grandma Mouse arrived, now who had time to fret about the weather?

"Nobody!" laughed Mother Mouse, sampling the frosting.

"Nobody!" laughed Father Mouse, dancing his little wife round and round the kitchen.

"Nobody!" laughed the sixteen sisters, mixing and beating and tasting. And they started to sing a little song.

April showers bring May flowers.
Squeakity, squeakity, squeak.
Everything's humming,
Grandma's coming.
Squeakity, squeakity ...!

"How?" said Napoleon.

The sixteen sisters stopped singing. Mother and Father Mouse stopped dancing. They all stared at Napoleon.

"How, what?"

"How's Grandma coming?" asked that worried little mouse. He pointed outside, and it looked as if his whiskers were starting to quiver.

At that, everybody ran to the window. Everybody's mouth went into a little round O. For the puddle had become a sea, and the sea had covered the field, and away off at the end of the field stood Grandma's house. From an upstairs window, someone was waving a hanky.

"Grandma!" choked all sixteen of the sister mice. They threw their pinafores over their heads and tried not to cry.

"Oh, dear, oh, dear, oh, dear!" whispered Mother Mouse. "Whatever shall we do?"

"Not a boat in the house," Father Mouse was muttering. "Not even an old inner tube!"

So busy were those sorry little mice, what with worrying and taking on, that nobody saw what Napoleon was doing. Nobody said, "Oh, no, it won't work!" or "Oh, no, it's too dangerous!"

By the time they did notice, that brave little mouse (along with the cake bowl and the wooden spoon) was halfway to Grandma's house, if you please, and paddling like nobody's business! His small mouse voice came back to them in a damp but happy song.

Hey for Grandma! Hey for me!
Hey for a life on the rolling sea!
Back we'll come in a one, two, three.
Oh, hey for the rolling, rolling, rolling,
Hey for the rolling sea!

Then everybody began to smile again, and hustle and bustle about. In a song and a dance and a one, two, three, everything was ready. The table was set, the snug little house was shiny clean. Wonderful smells came out of the kitchen ...

Then the rain began to stop and the sun began to shine. Before very long, back paddled Napoleon over the waves. There in the cake bowl beside him sat Grandma Mouse with her eyes as sparkly as the water all around them.

"A little rain never hurt anybody," she laughed, waving her hanky.

And "Happy Birthday, Grandma Mouse!" called Father and Mother Mouse and the sixteen sisters, waving back.

Then everybody looked at Napoleon as he came paddling up the path. So proud of him was that happy mouse family that nobody could think of a word to say about how wonderfully clever he was.

And that was just as well. Because if Napoleon had felt one smidgen happier, being so little and all, he would surely have burst. And that would never do on somebody's birthday! Now, would it?

THREE BOYS
IN A TREE

ONCE there were three boys who lived in a tree near the Jungle. Their names were DEAD-EYE DICK, THE SHADOW, and FIERCE FRED.

Way down in a hole at the bottom of the tree lived Dead-Eye Dick. Halfway up on a very big branch lived The Shadow. And Fierce Fred, who was smallest and hungriest, lived away up high against the sky at the tip-top of the tree.

10

All day long they played and they played, and they never, *never* NEVER went near the Jungle.

But one day Dead-Eye Dick grew tired of playing. "Let's go into the Jungle," said he, "and hunt for a Little Snack!"

So off they marched into the Jungle, one behind the other. As they marched, The Shadow beat his drum and they sang a song:

We're off to find a Snack, (BOOM!)
A hasty, tasty Snack, (BOOM!)
    But if we bungle
    In the Jungle,
We never may come back! (BOOM!)

Now they had not gone very far when they heard something behind them. THUMP, THUMP, THUMP...

They stopped right where they were.

"SH!" said Dead-Eye Dick, with his finger over his lips.

"SH!" said The Shadow, with his fingers in his ears.

"SOMETHING," said Fierce Fred, "is THUMPING..."

Slowly, they turned. They saw behind

11

them a PIGGYMOSSUM, who was also out hunting for a Little Snack in the Jungle! He was looking straight at them with a mean smile, and he was LICKING HIS CHOPS!

"Run, men!" called Dead-Eye Dick. And they ran and they ran back through the Jungle with the Piggymossum thumping close behind. With a ZIP! and a ZIP! and another ZIP! they popped into the hole at the bottom of the tree, just one thump ahead of the Piggymossum!

There in the cozy house of Dead-Eye Dick, the three boys had some ninny-cow tea and went to bed.

But the Piggymossum went and hid behind a tulip tree. There he stayed, all night long, getting hungrier and hungrier and meaner and meaner. As he got meaner, he planned a Little Plan. "I'll fix them!" said he with a mean smile.

Next day The Shadow popped out his head and looked around.

"All safe!" he called.

So out came the three boys, The Shadow and Fierce Fred and Dead-Eye Dick. As they marched off into the Jungle, one behind the other, they sang:

We're off to find a Snack, (BOOM!)
A nifty, swifty Snack, (BOOM!)
If something thumps,
Or growls, or jumps,
We'll soon be coming back! (BOOM!)

The mean old Piggymossum waited until they had gone. Then he crept up to their tree. He stuffed Dead-Eye Dick's house all full of dirt. Now there was no hole for them to run into. Then off went the Piggymossum into the Jungle to hunt for the three boys.

Now the boys had not gone very far when again they heard something. GUGGLETY, GUGGLETY, GUGGLETY . . .

"Sh!" they said. They turned to see who was going GUGGLETY behind them. This time it was a GUGGLY-UGLY, right at their heels! They ran straight to Dead-Eye Dick's hole and found it stuffed full. So ZIP! ZIP! ZIP! on they went to The Shadow's very big branch, halfway up the tree.

"That was a close one!" puffed The Shadow.

"They're getting bigger," puffed Dead-Eye Dick.

"I'm hungry," puffed Fierce Fred, "for a Little Snack."

13

But they had to be happy with ninny-cow tea, and then they went to bed. All night long the Guggly-Ugly hid behind the tulip tree, lashing his tail and guggling and thinking mean thoughts.

Next day, after the boys had left to hunt for a Little Snack in the Jungle, out he came. He crept straight up to their tree. He stretched on his hind legs as far as he could s-t-r-e-t-c-h. With his sharp teeth he cut through the very big branch that was The

Shadow's cozy house. Down it fell with a crash! Then, guggling meanly, off went the Guggly-Ugly into the Jungle to hunt for the three boys. (Remember, the Piggymossum was also out hunting for them!)

Now the three boys had not gone very far into the Jungle when they heard something behind them. Not THUMP. Not GUGGLETY. But CRASH, CRASH, CRASH! They turned on the spot, and they saw a ROARING SNERK, coming very fast and LICKING HIS CHOPS!

"Here we go again!" called Fierce Fred. And they ran and they ran as fast as they could run. They ran like the wind straight to their tree. On they went, past the stuffed-up hole that used to be Dead-Eye Dick's house, and on past the very big branch that used to be The Shadow's house and was not there any more. They went all the way up to Fierce Fred's house, high on the top of the tree. And there they sat, and panted.

Away down below, the Roaring Snerk sat and R-O-A-R-E-D.

"Ah!" panted Dead-Eye Dick.

"We made it!" panted The Shadow.

"Anyway," panted Fierce Fred, "I'm very hungry."

But once more, all they had was ninny-cow tea, this time way up high against the sky in Fierce Fred's cozy house.

"Do you know," whispered Fierce Fred, "that this can't go on much longer?"

"We know," said The Shadow and Dead-Eye Dick.

And then they went to bed.

But down below, the Roaring Snerk went and hid behind the tulip tree. All night long he waited, chewing on the tulips and roaring and thinking mean thoughts. In the morning, after the boys had left, out he crept. He started chewing through their tree. He chewed and he chewed, and soon the boy's tree shook a little. He chewed some more, until it waved back and forth. And some more, until it toppled over with a CRASH! that rang all over the Jungle.

Then the Snerk roared meanly. And off he went into the Jungle to hunt for the boys.

First he saw the hungry Guggly-Ugly, who was already hunting for the three boys. Next he saw the very hungry Piggymossum, who had been hunting for them even longer. They all crept nearer and nearer to where the three boys were marching along . . .

It was a lovely day in the Jungle. As the three boys marched along, they sang a little song:

> *We're off to find a Snack,* (BOOM!)
> *A yummy, hummy Snack,* (BOOM!)
>   *But if we see*
>   *The E-ne-my—*
> *We're going to hurry back!* (BOOM!)

Right in the middle of the last "BOOM!" they broke off. For suddenly they heard all three sounds at once. A THUMP! from this side! A GUGGLETY! from that! A CRASH, CRASH, CRASH! in the middle!

They ran and they ran out of the Jungle, back to their tree. But, as you know, the tree was not there any more, having been chewed down. So they ran like the wind right back into the Jungle again, in a big, fat circle. then The Shadow; and last of all, Fierce Fred, who was the smallest and hungriest.

Behind them came The Enemy. First the mean old Piggymossum, running as fast as he could run. Next, the Guggly-Ugly, running like anything, with his tail straight out behind. And last of all, the Roaring Snerk, running so fast that his ears turned outside-in. Out of the Jungle after the boys they ran, around the chewed-down tulip tree, and back into the Jungle again, in a big, fat circle.

And as they ran, they got to thinking . . .

The Snerk kept seeing the hind legs of the Guggly-Ugly just ahead. He kept thinking how much bigger the Guggly-Ugly was than the three boys all taken together. After a while he forgot about the boys and chased the

Guggly-Ugly instead, roaring loudly as he ran.

Now the Guggly-Ugly, who was running just behind the Piggymossum, was thinking along the same lines.

"What a very big Piggymossum that one is!" guggled he to himself. "The biggest I ever saw," he said. "Much the biggest!" And he forgot all about the three boys, and chased the Piggymossum instead.

The Piggymossum, now and then, looked behind him at both the Guggly-Ugly and the Snerk. Fierce Fred, who was just ahead, suddenly seemed very small. "Not worth the trouble," the Piggymossum said, with a mean smile.

And with that, the Piggymossum forgot the boys and headed for the Guggly-Ugly. At the same time, the Guggly-Ugly headed for the Piggymossum, and the Snerk headed for them both. Then all three came together with a BANG! that rang all over the Jungle . . . . .

That was the end of the mean old Piggymossum, and the Guggly-Ugly, and the Roaring Snerk.

But the three boys kept on running until they reached the Snack Bar on the other side

of the Jungle. There they had the Nicest Little Snack.

Under a balloon tree they ate hot dogs fried in butter, and potato chips, and chocolate ice-cream sodas. They ate all that they could hold. Dead-Eye Dick had ten Little Snacks. The Shadow had twenty Little Snacks. And Fierce Fred, who was smallest and hungriest, had one hundred and fifty-two. He put an extra one in his pocket for later on.

Then they marched back through the Jungle to make three new houses in the tulip tree: one low down for Dead-Eye Dick; one middle up for The Shadow; and one at the tiptop for Fierce Fred. (He was still the smallest, but he was not the hungriest any more.)

On their way they sang a little song:

We've had our Little Snack, (BOOM!)
Our super-duper Snack, (BOOM!)
  Now with a hop,
  A skip, and a jump,
We'd better be getting back! (BOOM!)

And that is all about Dead-Eye Dick, The Shadow, and Fierce Fred.

THE BUSY LITTLE BEAVERS

IN A SNUG little house in the middle of a pond, two young beavers were just waking up.

"Sun's out!" shouted Roger Beaver. "Today's the day!"

"What day?" yawned Billy.

"The day we visit Grandpa Beaver!" cried Roger, leaping out of bed.

Billy Beaver stopped yawning and began to smile. He began to think of the wonderful stories Grandpa told. And the little sailboats that Grandpa whittled. And the long, steep slide that led from Grandpa's front door straight down into the pond. Humming to himself, Billy hurried through his washing and scurried through his dressing.

Then he remembered something. Mother and Father Beaver loved to go to Grandpa's, too. But Father, of late, had been extremely busy, even with Mother Beaver to help him. "What about Father and Mother?" he asked.

"Father's too busy!" called Roger, already off to the kitchen.

Billy Beaver followed slowly. A little worried frown crept into his furry face. It was true. Father Beaver was as busy a beaver as you could hope to see.

"It's all because I'm so fond of my family," Father had told them only yesterday. He had jingled the pennies in his pockets and said proudly, "The best beaver dam! The snuggiest house! The fullest cupboard! *Nothing's* too fine for the fine family of Father Beaver!" And with that, off hurried this big, busy beaver to see about things. Like building up the beaver dam, stick by stick. Or fetching home wood for the winter, piece by piece. Or presenting his family with a nice bunch of water lily roots, root by root . . .

So with Father Beaver, thought Billy sadly. No time for rest. No time for play. No time, even, for a visit to Grandpa's!

But the minute Billy came into the kitchen, his eyes began to shine. His mouth began to water. For the yummiest smells were coming from the oven! The shelves were covered with bowls of berries and little heaps of sugar! Mother Beaver had on her prettiest party apron, and there was a big, secret smile on her face!

"Is it somebody's birthday?" Roger was asking.

"Guess again," said Mother Beaver.

Billy began to feel bubbly inside. He whispered, "Is it Christmas?"

"Not yet," smiled Mother Beaver.

"I know!" Roger shouted. *"It's Father's Day!"*

Mother Beaver nodded. As she beat the batter round and round, she sang a little song about the splendid things baking for the Father's Day dinner:

"Water lily popovers! Poplar steak!
Gooseberry dumplings! Blackberry cake!"
Those two young beavers smacked their lips and rubbed their furry stomachs just to think of it. Then they ate their breakfast. *Then* they brushed their teeth. And THEN they started off for Grandpa's. But they were still thinking about Father's Day.

Roger said, "Mother's getting Father a very special dinner for Father's Day."

Billy Beaver walked more slowly.

Roger said, "*We* didn't get Father *anything* for Father's Day."

Billy walked more slowly still.

"And we haven't any pennies," said Roger sadly, "to buy something with—"

Billy stopped. "We can make him a raft. With a raft, Father could carry *lots* of sticks to the dam—"

"—And *lots* of wood and roots to the house!" cried Roger. "*All at once!*"

Billy nodded. "Then he wouldn't be so busy. Then he could rest and play and go visit Grandpa!"

Roger turned a round, fat beaver somersault. "If we hurry," he cried, "we can finish the raft by dinner time!"

The sun rose high in the bright blue sky. It shone down on busy Father Beaver, towing his sticks, one by one, to the beaver dam. And on busy Mother Beaver, baking popovers and dumplings and huckleberry pie, as well. And on the two small beavers at the edge of the pond who were the busiest beavers of all! They cut and they measured. They nailed and they pounded. And, around dinner time, there was as pretty a raft as ever was made!

Those two young beavers (who had almost, but not quite forgotten about their visit to Grandpa's) sat back on their heels and looked at it proudly. They wrote some words on a piece of paper which they tied to the mast with a big red bow. *TO FATHER BEAVER* (said the words) *WITH A RAFT OF LOVE.* Then they anchored it right beside the front door, and waited.

Pretty soon Father Beaver came swimming home. When he saw the splendid raft, he said, "Well, well, well!" And he chuckled, "My, my, my!" He climbed aboard and he tried out the rudder and he patted the mast.

Then into the house hurried Father Beaver and whispered something to Mother Beaver, and they both hurried out again with big, heaped-up, steaming, mouth-watering baskets of food. Onto the raft went the Father's Day Dinner. And onto the raft went Father and Mother and Roger and Billy Beaver.

Then up with the anchor, and up with the sail, and across the pond floated those four smiling beavers! As they sailed along, they sang a merry song:

"Off to Grandpa's, you and I,
With cake and steak and huckleberry pie.
Sing Hi, sing Hey, we're on our way—
HIP, HIP, HOORAY FOR FATHER'S DAY!"

THE MAGIC UMBRELLA

Once there lived a kind little old school-
teacher by the name of Miss Mary Kilderry. She lived all by herself in the dearest
house that ever was. She had a little garden
and a monkey-puzzle tree.

Every day, as cheerful as a robin, off she

went and taught her twenty children in Grade Two. And at three o'clock, home she came. She tidied and she dusted and she baked gumdrop cookies, like any other little old lady.

And every night she washed up and put on her pink cotton nightie and her pink lace nightcap. She said her prayers and she went to sleep, just like any other nice little old lady.

But ONE warm night there was a ring around the moon. And this was the night that Miss Mary Kilderry turned into a fairy! Here is just what happened.

She was all ready for bed, nightcap and all. She opened her window and sat down on her window seat to worry. Every night for weeks and weeks Miss Mary Kilderry had sat by the window and worried about James Junior. James Junior could do ten-take-away-two and one-plus-four like nobody's business. But he did not believe in anything at all. He didn't believe in magic, and he didn't believe in fairies. Sometimes he didn't even believe in himself.

Miss Mary Kilderry sighed and sat, worrying and sniffing at the sweet night air.

"My, the garden smells pretty!" she said.

30

Right then she noticed something shining in the moonlight under the monkey-puzzle tree. It shone so brightly that Miss Mary was dazzled.

She blinked her eyes. "Now WHATEVER can it be?"

She hurried into her bathrobe and slippers, and she scurried out into her garden to see what wonderful thing shone out from the grass, brighter than fire.

Miss Mary was delighted. "Why, it's a wee umbrella," said she. "SOMEBODY TINY has gone off and left it!" And she bent down and picked it up.

As she did this, the strangest feeling went over her. It was a bubbly feeling, such as you get on a roller coaster, going down, or on Christmas Eve when you hear the chimes ringing. In fact, Miss Mary was sure that at this very moment she heard the loveliest music!

"Why, I do believe it's coming from the little umbrella," she said. So she opened it up to see. Then it happened! Before you could say "Mary Kilderry," she had turned into a fairy, as neat as you please. She was just the size of a brand-new pencil.

Along came a puff of wind. And up floated the tiny umbrella, carrying Miss Mary right along with it. Up and up she soared, with the pink ribbons of her nightcap floating along behind.

She watched her house and her garden and her monkey-puzzle tree grow smaller and smaller. She watched the stars in the Milky

Way grow larger and shiner. "Goodness gracious me!" said she. And, "Well, I NEVER!"

When Miss Mary's arms grew tired, she climbed up into the crook of the handle and sat down. Here she was very comfortable.

"I should have brought my papers to correct," she thought, for she always disliked to waste time.

Now she was passing at a great height over James Junior's house. Suddenly she had the loveliest idea. "We'll just show that young man a thing or two," she said to the umbrella. "Doesn't believe in magic, indeed! Why, the world is FULL of magic."

Down they floated until they were just outside James Junior's window. Peering in, Miss Mary Kilderry could see that her pupil was sound asleep.

She rapped sharply on the sill, and he opened one eye. Then, with a bound, he was at the window, both eyes as huge as picnic plates.

"Good evening, James Junior," said his teacher pleasantly.

James Junior blinked and stared and blinked again.

Miss Mary waggled her finger cheerfully.

"Come, James, speak when you're spoken to."

James Junior rubbed his eyes. "Miss Kilderry? It is you, isn't it, Miss Kilderry?"

"It most certainly is," she laughed. "Would you care to go for a little spin?"

He nodded, wondering at how very tiny his teacher had grown.

"Of course," she said practically, "you are much too big." She moved safely over the sill. "Just touch the umbrella," she told him.

Timidly James Junior touched the magic umbrella. Strange music swept past them like the wind. Instantly he himself was the size of a fairy. He fitted very nicely into the crook beside Miss Mary Kilderry, and up they both floated into the moonlight.

Just for the fun of it, they whirled in and out of a fat, moonlit cloud. Then they soared so high toward the Milky Way that they started to get the shivers and had to fly lower.

"We'd need space suits if we went any higher," called James Junior.

The wind whipped away his words and Miss Mary laughed with him.

Then they flew very low over town and pointed out the sleeping houses that belonged to the other second-graders.

After a while, James Junior got used to the idea of flying all over the sky in a shining umbrella. He even got used to the idea of being so very small. But he couldn't get used to one thought.

"Miss Kilderry," he said, as they reached his window, "are you truly a fairy?"

"Goodness gracious, no!" she laughed. "It's this umbrella. SOMEBODY forgot it and left it under my monkey-puzzle tree."

James Junior nodded as if it were all perfectly clear. "Probably a fairy, don't you suppose? Or a brownie. Or maybe it was an elf."

"Why, who knows?" asked his teacher brightly. "Now I must hurry along home. It's going to rain tomorrow and SOMEBODY will be needing this umbrella."

James Junior climbed over the window sill. As big as ever, he nodded again. "Well, anyhow, now I'll believe anything."

Miss Mary Kilderry waved good night and floated away with a little secret smile.

She made a perfect landing under the monkey-puzzle tree. When she stepped out of the magic umbrella, she became her own comfy size again. And then she folded the umbrella and left it exactly where she had found it.

In the morning, sure enough, the rain was splashing down into the lilacs. Before schooltime, Miss Mary Kilderry put on her rubbers and hurried out into the garden. Just as she thought, SOMEBODY had come and taken away the little umbrella!

But under the monkey-puzzle tree there glowed for a whole week the brightest spot of magic that anyone ever saw.

CHUGGER

ONCE there was a toy train named Chugger. One morning Chugger opened his eyes. Everything looked strange. "I'm not in Tommy's room," he said. "Where am I?"

A little chickadee was hunting for bugs nearby.

"Good morning, Mrs. Chickadee," said Chugger. "Can you tell me where I am?"

"Chick-a-dee-dee-dee, you are in the field," said Mrs. Chickadee. "It's too bad, but Tommy forgot you."

"Forgot me!" said Chugger.

"He has gone to the seashore," said Mrs. Chickadee, hopping about.

"To the seashore!" said Chugger. "But what shall I do all summer?"

"Dear me," said Mrs. Chickadee. "I have so MUCH to do, I can't think. I must hunt for some bugs for my four babies who are waiting at home, all alone."

And off flew Mrs. Chickadee to hunt for some bugs for her babies.

"Oh, dear," said Chugger. "I must go hunt for something to do all summer until Tommy comes back."

CHUG-CHUG-CHUG, off rolled Chugger across the field. Soon he met a hen.

"Good morning, Mrs. Hen," said Chugger. "Tommy has gone to the seashore. Can you tell me what to do all summer?"

"Cluck-a-cluck," said Mrs. Hen. "I have so MUCH to do, I can't tell you, Chugger. I must hunt for some grain for my three chicks to eat. They are waiting at home, all alone."

And away ran Mrs. Hen to hunt for some grain for her babies.

CHUG-CHUG-CHUG, off rolled Chugger into the woods. Soon he met a squirrel.

"Good morning, Mrs. Squirrel," said Chugger. "Tommy has gone to the seashore. What shall I do all summer? Can you help me?"

"Chit-chit-chit," said Mrs. Squirrel. "I have so MUCH to do, I can't help you, Chugger. I have to hunt for some nuts for my two baby squirrels to eat. They are waiting at home, all alone."

And off ran Mrs. Squirrel to hunt for some nuts for her babies.

CHUG-CHUG-CHUG, off rolled Chugger through the woods, feeling very lonesome. Soon he met a fox.

"Good morning, Mrs. Fox," said Chugger. "Tommy has gone away to the seashore and left me. What shall I do all summer? Can you help me?"

"Yap-yap-yap," barked Mrs. Fox. "I have so MUCH to do, I can't help you, Chugger. I must hunt for some berries for my baby fox to eat. He is waiting at home, all alone." And off trotted Mrs. Fox to hunt for some berries for her baby.

Chugger blinked his eyes. He felt so alone. And he had nothing to do today. He had nothing to do all summer long.

Suddenly he heard a loud NOISE. "Chugger!" the noise called. "Chugger!"

First it was Mrs. Chickadee. "Chick-a-dee-dee-dee," she said. "I can help you."

Then it was Mrs. Hen. "Cluck-a-cluck," said Mrs. Hen. "I can, too."

"Chit-chit-chit," said Mrs. Squirrel. "I can, too."

"Yap-yap-yap," barked Mrs. Fox. "So can I."

And what do you think they all had with them? They all had their babies, every one. And what do you think they did? They put their babies into Chugger's little cars!

Into his black coal car went the four happy baby chickadees. They were all talking at once. "Chick-a-dee-dee-dee-dee," said all the baby birds.

Into his green passenger car went the three baby chicks. "Cheep-cheep-cheep," said all the baby chicks, as gay as you please.

Into his blue freight car went the two merry baby squirrels. "Chit-chit, chit-chit," said the baby squirrels.

And last of all, into Chugger's red caboose went the little fox, as pleased as he could be. "Yap-yap-yap," barked the baby fox.

"While we are hunting for something to eat," said Mrs. Chickadee and Mrs. Hen and Mrs. Squirrel and Mrs. Fox, "would you be our baby sitter? And you may live with us until Tommy comes back."

"Yes, thank you," said Chugger. "Now I have SOMETHING BIG to do all summer."

CHUG-CHUG-CHUG, off they went for a ride. Off they went with a very merry "Toot-toot-toot."

And a "Chick-a-dee-dee-dee."

And a "Cheep-cheep-cheep."

And a "Chit-chit-chit."

And a "Yap-yap-yap."

41

THE HOLE IN THE GROUND

ONCE upon a time there was a little hole in the ground. It was a deep, round hole, and it was new. Somebody had dug it underneath the winterberry tree. But no one knew who. Somebody had planted bluebells all around the hole in a pretty circle. Somebody had made the nicest little path between two rows of buttercups. And somebody had put up a letter box. It was made out of an empty puffball, and it had a name printed on it. But nobody could read the name, so nobody knew who had done all this. Nobody could guess who lived in the hole underneath the winterberry tree.

Along came a fat and jolly wiggleworm. He looked at the name on the letter box. It meant nothing at all to him, except maybe little worm tracks.

"Maybe a nice fat worm like me lives here," he said. "I'll go and see."

So he wiggled up the path between the buttercups. He poked his head into the hole, the small, deep, round hole. He called out in his whispery worm's voice,

> *Hello! Hello!*
> *Who lives below?*

He listened and he listened. But he heard only the wind singing in the bluebells. He heard no jolly worm wiggling down there in the hole. So home he went, down the path between the buttercups. He forgot to eat his supper. All he did was sit and wonder:

> *Who lives in the hole,*
> *The brand-new hole,*
> *The deep, round hole*
> *By the winterberry tree?*

After a while a sleepy old mole came poking by. He squinted at the squiggles on the letter box for a long time to see if they said "mole."

"Maybe they do and maybe they don't," said he. "I'll go and see."

So up the path went the sleepy old mole. He poked his head into the hole. It was nice and dark down there. He called in his creaky mole's voice,

Is it a mole
Who owns this hole?

He listened for a long time. But all he heard was the wind in the bluebells. He heard no sleepy mole digging down in the hole. So he went away home. And all he did when he got there was sit and wonder:

Who lives in the hole,
The brand-new hole,
The deep, round hole
By the winterberry tree?

Pretty soon a cottontail bunny came hoppity-hopping along. He saw the new hole in the ground. He saw the ring of bluebells and the buttercup path. With his ruby eyes he stared at the letters on the puffball letter box. His nose twitched and twitched.

"Maybe what it says is 'bunny,'" he decided. "I'll go see."

So hoppity-hop up the path went the cottontail bunny. He poked his twitchity nose into the hole—the small, deep, round hole.

Halloo! Halloo!
Are you a bunny too?

He held one floppy ear close to the hole. Perhaps he would hear a twitchity bunny nose, twitching down there in the hole. But there was only the wind in the bluebells. And the hole was very dark. He hopped home as fast as he could go. And there he sat, and worried and worried:

Who lives in the hole,
The brand-new hole,
The deep, dark hole
By the winterberry tree?

After a while the wind was still. The sun went to bed behind the hill. Everything was quiet.

Suddenly down the path came a whistle and a hum. It went something like this:

Whistle-whistle-whistle,
Tiddle-um-tum,
Hustle and a bustle,
And a go and a come,
And a whistle-whistle-whistle
And a tiddle-um-tum!

Who should skip down the path but a lively elf! He ran straight to his letter box and looked in. His whistle and his hum stopped short.

"No mail again today," he said sadly. "None of my old friends write to me. Nobody new ever comes to see me."

The poor little elf picked up his pail of strawberries. Scuffing his toes, he started up his path between the buttercups. He was looking at the ground, the way you do when you are sad.

That is how he saw the tracks. He saw

the track of a jolly worm, going calling. He saw the track that a sleepy mole makes when looking for another sleepy mole. He saw the track made by a hoppity bunny who has just found nobody at home.

What do you suppose that the lively elf did then? Why, he hustled and he bustled in his cozy house under the ground. He set the table with his very best bluebell dishes. He set out grass tidbits for a jolly wiggleworm. And bugs for a sleepy mole. And clover for a hoppity bunny. And fat red strawberries and milkweed cream for a lively elf—who was himself.

Then, whistling and humming, away he went to find his new friends—the worm, the mole and the bunny. There they were, all sitting in their holes. They were all sitting and wondering who lived in the new hole nearby.

When they saw who it was, they were just as pleased as they could be. Wouldn't you like to have supper with the lively elf who lives in the hole by the winterberry tree? I would.

And so did the jolly worm, the sleepy mole and the hoppity bunny.

THE COCOA-COLORED BEAR
WHO WOULD NOT
BRUSH HIS HAIR

IN THE Deep Deep Woods lived a little bear,
just the color of cocoa. When Mother Bear
nuzzled him around his cocoa ears, like this,
he smelled as fuzzy and warm as a baby
kitten. When Father Bear gave him a big
bear-hug, like this, he laughed and said,
"WOO-OOF!" Wouldn't you think that a little
cocoa-colored bear THAT soft and cuddly
would also be quite perfect?

But no. He was not. Something was terribly wrong. It is true that he cleaned his teeth carefully every day on fern roots. He came to all his meals on time, especially when there was honey. He went to bed the minute he was called, curling up all soft in the sleeping corner of the cave. BUT—the little cocoa-colored bear would never brush his hair!

Underneath all that soft fuzziness were tangles and snarls, and horrid floo-floo nests! And day by day it got worse and worse.

Mother Bear would call, "Hairbrushing time!"

And the little bear would say, "No, it hurts," and keep right on playing.

Father Bear would say, "Only little bears who brush their hair can go on hunting trips for honey."

And the little bear would say, "No, it pulls," and run away.

One warm day Mother Bear and Father Bear each took one of his soft round paws, and they started off through the Deep Deep Woods.

The little cocoa-colored bear, never suspecting a thing, hopped up and down merrily between them, singing a gay song:

We're go-ing to the village!
We're go-ing to the town!
We're go-ing to buy a lollipop,
All choco-late brown!

When the bears reached town, they strolled into a shop with a peppermint-pole upright beside the door. "The candy shop!" thought the cocoa-colored little bear happily.

But it was not a candy shop. A man in a white smock led the little bear to a big white chair. He took up some clippers. He looked at Father and Mother Bear.

Father and Mother Bear nodded. "From head to toe," they sighed.

Soon the little bear was not cocoa-colored any longer. He was pink and smooth.

"Anyway, it's a warm day," thought the little bear as they left. "My, how all these people stare, now that I'm a bare bear!"

They bought a cocoa-colored lollipop at the candy shop. As he ate it, on the way home through the Deep Deep Woods, the little pink bear was very thoughtful.

Every day for a week he got up early and brushed his skin for ten minutes—just to help the fur come in.

On Monday a tiny bit of cocoa-colored fuzz appeared! He brushed for twenty minutes.

On Tuesday, the fuzz was long enough to see—oh, very faintly! He brushed for half an hour.

And a week later it was long enough to gleam from the brushing, like chocolate icing on pink frosting. He brushed all day!

Mother Bear suggested gently, "I think one hundred strokes a day will be enough from now on."

And Father Bear took the little cocoa-colored bear on a hunting trip for honey!

ANDREW THE KANGAROO

ANDREW was a young kangaroo who lived
in the Bush. He LOOKED like all the
other kangaroos in Australia. He had long
soft eyes in his small head. He had dainty
forelegs, and strong hind legs built for getting about in leaps. He had a lovely big tail
to balance himself with. But Andrew was
DIFFERENT.

One day he grew too big to be carried any
longer in his mother's pouch.

"Now you must hop about, yourself, Andrew," Mother Kangaroo told him fondly.

"Just do as we do," said Father Kangaroo, taking a big hop.

Andrew tried. He did exactly what kangaroos always do when they jump. But Andrew, every time he tried it, went OOMP, flat on his face.

This made all the Relatives gather round in wonder, clicking their tongues.

"Do it this way," said his mother, sailing up and down with big graceful leaps.

"This way," called his father, making upside-down scallops through the air.

"This way," cried the Relatives, bouncing high in all directions.

"Oh, THAT way," said Andrew. He tried again. And again. And every time he did, he went OOMP, flat on his shiny little nose.

After a while the Relatives shook their heads sadly.

"He'll never do," sighed one uncle.

"He'll never be able to get his own food," sighed a great-aunt.

"He'll never get to enter the Jumping Contest," cried one of the cousins.

"Never mind," said Father Kangaroo

cheerfully, "I'll hop around and do the shopping."

Mother Kangaroo smiled. "If Andrew can't leap like other kangaroos, he'll just have to be extra good at everything else. We'll make the best of what we have."

And since Andrew was what they had, they made the best of him.

His mother taught him to be the best-mannered and the kindest young kangaroo in the Bush.

His father found him the finest green plants. He taught him how to build up his muscles by kicking and rolling. Soon he was also the healthiest and the strongest young kangaroo in the Bush.

Now and then the Relatives came to see if he had learned to jump. Andrew just smiled at them politely from his favorite spot under the bunya-bunya tree. Sometimes he whittled them trinkets and tops.

"Andrew is different from the others," they sighed.

"Certainly he is," his mother and his father would say proudly. "Andrew is no ordinary kangaroo."

They were right.

The day before the Jumping Contest, Andrew wrote a note to his family: I AM GOING INTO THE JUNGLE TO MAKE SOMETHING. LOVE, ANDREW.

Then he took his whittling knife, and he kicked and rolled through the grass and into the jungle.

When his mother and father and all the Relatives came back from their feeding grounds, they found the note under the bunya-bunya tree.

"Andrew is unhappy about not being in the Jumping Contest," sighed the uncle.

"Poor boy," sighed the great-aunt.

"At least he should have stayed to watch us," cried the cousins.

But Andrew's mother and father just smiled. "Andrew is making the best of it," they said.

And he was.

Next day all the young kangaroos—excepting Andrew, of course—gathered for the Jumping Contest.

Such jumps as they jumped! One kangaroo jumped a terrific jump from here to there. Another kangaroo jumped from there way over to there.

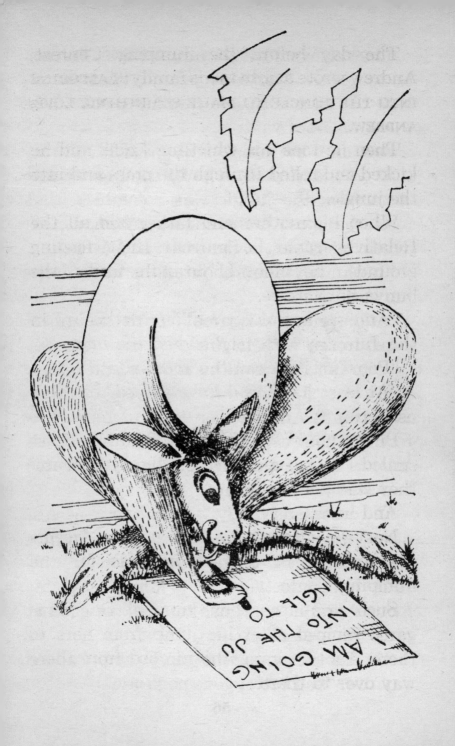

They all would have jumped even farther except that everyone missed Andrew so badly, sitting in his old familiar place under the bunya-bunya tree.

Suddenly the judge said, "Wait!"

Everyone turned. There, coming toward them from the jungle was Something that took the most tremendous, enormous, gigantic leaps that a kangaroo had ever seen.

"It's an airplane!" shouted the uncle, leaping with fright.

"It's a giant kangaroo!" cried the great-aunt, frozen with fright.

"It's ANDREW!" said his mother and father. "On a pogo stick!"

Of course Andrew won the Jumping Contest. Without even stopping for a breath, he jumped higher and farther than a kangaroo had ever jumped before.

Of course everybody was as happy as Andrew, because they loved him. And Andrew was the happiest kangaroo in the Bush.

"A kangaroo who can't jump," said his mother and father, "has to be extra good at everything else."

"And a kangaroo who can't jump," added Andrew, "had better get a pogo stick!"

THE NAUGHTY LITTLE TIGER

ONCE upon a time there were three little tigers. Two were as nice as nice could be. But the third was simply terrible, he was so naughty.

One morning Mrs. Tiger said, "Hunting time!"

The two little tigers trotted off nicely behind her to where the tall grass grows.

But the third said, "Huh!" And didn't he drag his toes all the way to the meadow? Indeed he did.

"Sh!" said Mrs. Tiger. "Just wait here."

The two little tigers sat down in the hot sun to wait, as nice as nice could be.

But the naughty tiger looked toward the cool, green jungle. Then he looked toward Mrs. Tiger. All he could see above the grass was the tip of her golden tail. Then he looked at his two brothers. Said that naughty little tiger, "Coming?"

So the three little tigers trotted off all alone into the cool, green jungle. Here it was, as dark and as still as the night. Tiptoe, tiptoe, went the three little tigers down the path. Soon they came to a pool.

"Listen!" whispered the first little tiger. All three put their heads to one side and listened to the footsteps coming toward them.

"Look!" whispered the second little tiger. All three looked, and their eyes grew very green. For there stood a tall, tall something with a long, long neck and two short horns. And it was as tall as a tree!

"H-hello," said the two little tigers, as nice as nice could be.

But the naughty little tiger made his most terrible face and snarled his meanest snarl and moved his tail slowly from side to side.

"What dreadful manners!" sniffed the tall something. She handed one of the nice tigers a lovely, bumpy bundle. "Please take this home to your mother and tell her 'thank you' for me." Then off she trotted.

After a minute, on crept the three little tigers, deep into the jungle, tiptoe, tiptoe. Two little tigers looked back over their shoulders now and then. But the naughty little tiger trotted straight on. Soon they came to another pool.

"Smell!" whispered the first little tiger. All three raised their noses and sniffed at an animal smell coming toward them.

"Look!" whispered the second little tiger. All three looked, and their eyes grew very round. For there stood a big, big something with a long, long, long nose, and feet like hairy stumps. And it was as big as a jungle!

"H-hello," said the two little tigers, as nice as nice could be.

But the naughty little tiger saw the bumpy bundle carried by this big something, so he did not act quite so terrible as before. He just growled and spit and made a dreadful face. He was pretty awful, just the same.

"Such manners!" sniffed the big something. And she gave her bundle to the two nice tigers. "Please tell your mother 'thank you' for me." And she trotted off, leaving the three little tigers all alone in the jungle.

"I want to go home," said the first little tiger, thoughtfully sniffing at his bundle.

"Me, too," said the second little tiger, deciding that his bundle smelled delicious.

And the only-a-little-bit-naughty tiger said, "Well....."

But right before them stood a very terrible something, with two big horns on the end of his nose, and two wicked eyes. And he looked much more terrible than the naughty little tiger sometimes acted. He licked his lips, and he smiled a terrible smile.

The three little tigers turned and ran, past the black pools, out of the green jungle, and straight toward Mrs. Tiger's big, golden arms. And that terrible little tiger—whose terribleness had all gone out of him—ran the fastest and got there first.

Mrs. Tiger looked hard at her three naughty children. She looked hardest of all at her third little tiger. Then she hugged them hard.

You must have met that terrible-looking Mr. Rhinoceros," she said. "Now maybe you will wait when I tell you to."

Then she opened the two bumpy bundles. "Well, well! Here is the sugar that Mrs. Giraffe borrowed last Tuesday. And here is the mincement that Mrs. Elephant borrowed last Monday. Well, well, well!"

So Mrs. Tiger baked a big, round, golden mince pie, of course. And the three little tigers, just as nice as nice could be, ate all that they could hold.

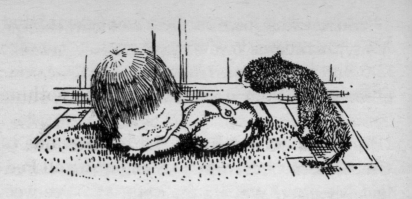

THE PRETEND PONY

THERE once was a boy named Pee-wee who wanted a pony so much that he could think of nothing else.

"Come to supper!" his mother would call.

Pee-wee washed his hands and sat down at the table nicely enough. But right away he started thinking about that pony. Soon his supper was stone-cold, and everybody else was finished.

"Bedtime, Pee-wee," his father would say. Pee-Wee started off well enough by cleaning his teeth and scrubbing his ears. But sooner or later he began thinking about the pony. There they would find him in the morning, sound asleep on the rug, with his clothes still on and a wishful smile on his face.

"Something has to be done about that pony," said Pee-Wee's mother.

"But not this year," said Father.

So they shook their heads and did nothing about the pony at all.

Soon Pee-wee's jolly Uncle Wally came to visit. When he saw that the pony was all Pee-wee could think about, he said, "Pee-wee, you just PRETEND you have that pony. If you pretend a thing hard enough, sometimes it comes true."

Pee-wee grew excited for the first time in weeks. "How long will it take?" he cried.

Jolly Uncle Wally scratched his head. "Oh, I should say maybe three days."

"Now, Wally," said Pee-wee's mother.

But Pee-wee got right to work. First of all, he had to have a pony shed. The old woodshed would do, Pee-wee decided. All that first morning he worked. He cleaned out the shed and swept it carefully. He nailed down planks to mend the floor. He tacked tarpaper onto the roof to keep the pony dry. And all the time he worked, Pee-wee pretended that the pony was right outside, grazing in the grass.

When they called him to supper, Pee-wee

rode fast across the field on the pretend pony. He reached the house a great deal sooner than ever before.

"How strange!" said Pee-wee's mother, watching at the window. "Pee-wee seems to be several feet off the ground!"

"So he does," said Father, peering. "That boy is pretending that pony so hard, I can almost see it myself!"

Jolly Uncle Wally just puffed on his pipe.

That was the first day.

On the second day, Pee-wee built the pony stall. For the walls, he used some old planks that were out behind the shed. After that, he built a fine feed bin, just as high as a pony's nose. Next he built a shelf to hold the water pail. And all day long, as hard as he worked,

Pee-wee pretended even harder. He pretended that his pony was grazing just outside the shed, and that he was brown with maybe a white star on his soft nose.

When they called him to supper, Pee-wee untied the pretend pony. He clucked his tongue and galloped to the house in less time than it takes to tell about it.

Father blinked his eyes. "Must need glasses," he said. "Pee-wee seems to be several feet off the ground again."

"Not only that," whispered Pee-wee's mother. "He appears to be mounted on SOMETHING BROWN!"

Pee-wee tied the pretend pony to the porch rail and came in, not one bit out of breath. Jolly Uncle Wally gave Pee-wee a broad wink, and kept on puffing his pipe.

That was the second day.

On the third and last day, Pee-wee worked hard to put up a fence. All that morning, jolly Uncle Wally helped him. But he had to go away for a while, so Pee-Wee finished the fence by himself. Last of all, he filled the pony's water pail and fed him.

But not for a minute did Pee-wee forget to pretend. He pretended that the brown pony with the white star on his nose was just outside, grazing in the field. He even pretended that his brown pony had a golden tan cowboy saddle with a new rope coiled on the pommel. He pretended harder than ever before. He pretended so hard that his hair felt tight around his head.

When they called him to supper, Pee-wee went outside the shed. Sure enough, just as jolly Uncle Wally had said, the pony had come true! He was soft brown, with a white star on his nose, and he wore a golden tan cowboy saddle with a new rope coiled on the pommel. Pee-wee stroked the pony's neck. His coat was soft and his breath was warm and sweet.

Pee-wee's mother and father looked out of the window and their eyes grew very round. "A brown pony with a saddle," Mother whispered. "I never would have believed it!"

Father shook his head. "I still don't," he said.

Jolly Uncle Wally walked across the field, puffing on his pipe. Proudly, Pee-wee rode up to him. "Looks like I pretended hard enough, doesn't it?" he said.

"Looks that way," smiled Uncle Wally.

THE ELEPHANT WHOSE
EARS WERE COLD

Now once there was a little gray elephant with big gray elephant ears. All day long in the nice, warm jungle Little Elephant dashed about with his big gray ears going flip-flap-flop. He was the happiest little elephant. Everybody loved to see him coming.

But sometimes the jungle nights were chilly. Then the little gray elephant was miserable.

"My ears are cold," said he to himself one chilly night. "And there is so MUCH of them to get c-cold."

First he tried to cover them with his trunk. But his trunk covered only one ear at a time. And when that ear was as warm as toast, the other one was all over shivers.

Then he tried to cover his ears with his tail. Round and round he turned. But no matter how fast he went, his tail never came anywhere near his ears.

"My ears are all g-goose flesh," he whispered to himself. "And I can't sleep a wink."

So when morning came, Little Elephant was as sleepy as a cat. He didn't dash happily through the jungle with his ears going flip-flap-flop. He just dragged his toes, and grumbled.

Soon he met Lester Lion, who was looking very rested.

"GOOD morning," sang Lester. "It's a LOVELY day."

"Lovely," grumbled Little Elephant, yawning widely.

"What, SLEEPY?" asked Lester.

"My ears," explained Little Elephant. "They get so cold at night I can't sleep a wink."

"That's EASY," laughed Lester Lion "Grow some fur on them, like mine."

70

That night Little Elephant brushed his ears and brushed his ears. And in the morning there they were, just as bare as ever. Not a smidgen of fur in sight. Little Elephant dragged his toes through the jungle, thinking and thinking.

"Good morning," sang out Smiley Crocodile.

"Morning," muttered Little Elephant.

Smiley grinned. "You look sleepy. Too bad to be sleepy on a splendid day like this."

"My ears are so cold at night," yawned Little Elephant, "I can't sleep a wink."

"Then why don't you sleep in the river?" said Smiley. "Like me."

With a tremendous splash, Smiley Crocodile dived into the river and didn't come up.

That night Little Elephant went to bed in the warm river. He found a nice soft mud bar to sit on, and he left the top of his trunk sticking out above water. Then he closed his tired eyes.

BUMP! A sleepy crocodile bumped him on the left. BUMP! A sleepy water buffalo bumped him on the right. Then two sleepy hippopotamuses bumped him in the middle. BUMP! BUMP!

71

Little Elephant came out of the river to yawn. And when he did, he stayed out. And when he stayed out, his ears were colder than ever, because they were all wet.

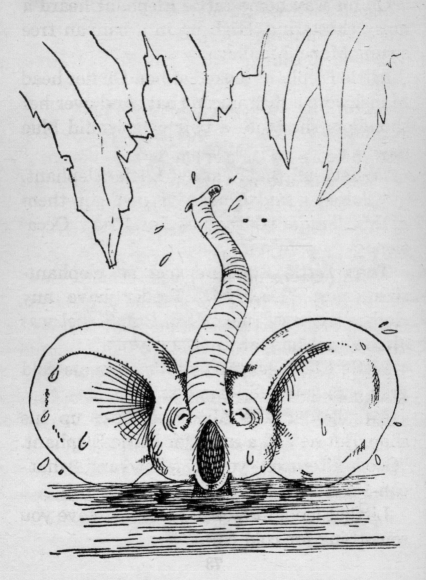

"Dearodearodearodear!" blinked Little Elephant. And he flopped his ears to get some feeling into them.

"Might as well go home," he sighed.

On his way home Little Elephant heard a noisy chattering. High up in a banyan tree swung Mabel Monkey.

Little Elephant looked at her. On her head Mabel wore a magnificent hat. And over her shoulders she wore a pair of splendid blue pajamas.

"What's all that?" asked Little Elephant.

"Clothes," said Mabel. "I just got them at Mr. Trader's—'Clothes For Every Occasion.'"

Then Little Elephant had an elephant-sized idea. "Does Mr. Trader have any clothes for EARS?" he called. But Mabel was already ten banyan trees away.

Little Elephant started out with his cold gray ears going flip-flap-flop.

Mr. Trader was about to close up his shop. But he had a smile for Little Elephant. "Good-afternoon-young-fellow-and-what-can-I-do-for-you?"

Little Elephant looked around. "Have you something for cold ears?"

"We have just the thing," said Mr. Trader. And he handed Little Elephant something for cold ears. "Ear muffs," he smiled. "Try 'em on."

Poor Little Elephant. The lovely furry ear muffs would not go over his head at all. Though they did fit the tip of his trunk very nicely.

"I'm sorry," said Little Elephant politely, blinking away a tear. "That part of me never gets cold."

"Hmmmmm," said Mr. Trader. "Just wait here a minute."

Little Elephant waited and waited. He heard sounds coming from the house. Then he closed one eye to rest it. Then he closed the other to rest IT. Then he heard Mr. Trader say, "Wake up, Little Elephant. Here you are."

Little Elephant opened his eyes. There stood Mr. Trader and his wife. And in Mrs. Trader's hand was the biggest, fuzziest, softest, comfiest pair of ear muffs anybody had ever seen anywhere. They were made of white fluffy lamb's wool, and they were HUGE. Just the size of Little Elephant's floppy gray ears.

"Try 'em on!" beamed Mr. Trader.

Down over his ears they went, those elephant ear muffs, just as slick as a whistle.

"A perfect fit," laughed Mrs. Trader, clapping her hands.

"Time for bed," laughed Little Elephant. He kissed Mrs. Trader thank you. Then he shook hands with Mr. Trader. Then home through the jungle he dashed, as happy as could be.

And his big gray elephant ears were so snug inside those woolly ear muffs that he yawned. And he yawned. And he yawned. And he slept until eleven o'clock in the morning—right through breakfast.

THE SCHOOL IN THE POOL

NOW BENJAMIN BEAVER was a very fine fellow. Nothing pleased him more than to do a good deed for others, be it giving to the Animal Red Cross, or working on the Community Dam in the pool where he lived. A good idea of any kind made Benjamin beam all over his furry face.

One morning at breakfast he began to smile. "That's it!" he cried. "That's just what we animals need!"

"What is?" asked Mrs. Beaver fondly.

"A school!" Benjamin pushed back his chair and paced up and down. "I can see it now! We'll have it in the empty beaver lodge out in the middle of the Pool! We'll build a little bridge to it for the animals who can't swim! We'll hire a teacher from the city! We'll—"

"What is a school?" asked Mrs. Beaver timidly.

"A school, my dear," declared Benjamin, snapping his suspenders, "is a place to learn things! Everyone likes to learn things!"

Mrs. Beaver nodded dreamily. "I'd like to learn to make dumplings like Mrs. Rabbit's."

"You see?" chuckled Benjamin. "And I'd give anything to learn to dive like Grandpa Otter!"

Yes, indeed. A school in the Pool was just what was needed! Benjamin Beaver hurried off to see if the neighbors thought so, too.

First he called on the Robert Rabbits, who lived in a damp hole nearby. They and their two dozen children were plugging up leaks in the roof with herb dumplings.

"A school!" they cried, and their eyes shone just like pink beads.

"*Then* we could learn to build better, like beavers," said Robert Rabbit, blushing a little.

"You see, the rain comes in sometimes," explained Mrs. Rabbit shyly.

"School begins tomorrow!" promised Benjamin. "Nine o'clock sharp!"

On around the Pool went that good beaver, humming to himself. Everywhere, he found the neighbors all excited about learning new things. Grandpa Otter wanted to learn some fishing tricks, such as those used by Barnaby Bear. Barnaby Bear, on the other hand, hoped to learn more about food. (There was, indeed, so much of him to feed.)

So it went. Benjamin Beaver headed for home in splendid spirits. On the way, he stopped to build a pretty little bridge to the schoolhouse in the middle of the Pool. Then he burst into his house and shouted, "We've done it! We have a fine school for learning things! And some fine pupils to learn them!"

Mrs. Beaver smiled proudly at her husband. "And a fine teacher to teach them?"

"What did you say?"

Mrs. Beaver repeated, "Do we have a teacher to teach them?"

78

Benjamin Beaver hurried to the telephone. He rang up the city. "We need a teacher right away," he explained. "Someone for cooking and diving and building and fishing."

"Dear me!" said the voice in the telephone. "That sort of teacher is what we're fresh out of. There isn't a one to be had!"

Benjamin hung up. "I could teach the class in building, myself. I'd like that. But what about the cooking class? And the diving class? And the fishing class?" A large tear tumbled down Benjamin's furry cheek. "I guess a school wasn't such a good idea, after all."

Right then, Mrs. Beaver had the loveliest thought. Without a word to her husband, she donned her shawl and hurried throughout the neighborhood.

Next morning, a little before nine o'clock, Mrs. Beaver said, "Time for school!"

"But," said Benjamin, "you can't have a school without a teacher."

"Come along, anyway," said Mrs. Beaver, smiling a secret smile. So off they hurried, around the Pool and across the bridge, and they reached the schoolhouse just in time.

Benjamin Beaver stared and stared. There were all the good neighbors, ready and waiting, scrubbed and combed and eager to learn!

"But where is the teacher?" asked Benjamin Beaver.

"We're ALL going to be teachers!" they laughed.

And so they were. That whole wonderful

morning they taught, and they learned—all kinds of things. Barnaby Bear gave everyone a thrilling fishing lesson. Grandpa Otter's diving class became extremely noisy and exciting. Benjamin himself conducted the course in building, with a picnic table as the first lesson.

By popular demand, Mrs. Rabbit taught the cooking class. It ended just at noontime and the new picnic table was covered with bowls of steaming chowder and rich herb dumplings, with platters of crunchy salads and dozens of juicy pies!

Between the first course and the second, everybody decided that the school was Benjamin's best idea yet, and that nobody would ever miss a day of it. After dessert, the two dozen young rabbits stood up and sang a song they had written. It went like this:

"We love learning something new,
Building, diving, cooking, too—
Hooray for the teachers! Hooray
for the Pool!
Give three cheers for the brand
new school!"

And everybody did give three cheers, especially Benjamin Beaver!

GABRIEL

THERE was an old house on the edge of town belonging to Mr. and Mrs. Gould. Right in the middle of the house there was a little tower. In this little tower lived Gabriel, a small and friendly ghost.

The Goulds had had Gabriel a long time without even knowing it, and Gabriel loved them very much. He spent every minute with them that he could spare from haunting his tower.

So that is how Gabriel knew about birthdays. The mysterious packages hidden under the bed! The secret swishes of tissue paper! The yummy cake and the shining candles and the dishes of ice cream and the splendid paper streamers in the dining room! And, best of all, the boys and girls from town who came tiptoeing in at the back door to make it a surprise!

Twice a year all these wonderful things happened, once for Mrs. Gould and once for Mr. Gould. Just thinking about it made Gabriel go tingly all over, with chills up and down the back and happy shivers in the tummy. Finally he could stand it no longer.

"You know what?" Gabriel said to his friend, Owl, who lived in a tree outside his window. "I'm going to have me a birthday!"

"Ghosts," hooted Owl, "don't have birthdays!"

"This one does!" said Gabriel firmly.

"Hmmm," said Owl. "When?"

Gabriel thought very hard. Then he hunted all through the calendar. At last he smiled a faraway smile. "I'll know," said Gabriel, "by the yummy smells in the kitchen and the splendid streamers in the dining room. And the things under the bed. And mostly, I'll know by the children, whispering all over town!"

"Maybe," said Owl.

That was in the summer. As excited as a secret, Gabriel waited for his birthday, crossing the days off the calendar one by one. The weeks went by and fall came and the leaves fell, red and gold. The children piled them high and jumped into them. Mr. Gould raked them over his rose beds. Mrs. Gould finished her fall cleaning.

"Had your birthday yet?" Owl asked Gabriel.

"No-o," said Gabriel, "but I will soon." And he crossed off another day. "Maybe," thought Gabriel, "it will be tomorrow." But no, there had not been a single swish of tissue paper, not even a smell of chocolate cake. "Maybe they're making it a surprise," thought Gabriel. But no, he had not noticed a thing under the bed. Nowhere around town had there been a whisper or a tiptoe. "Maybe," said Gabriel slowly, "maybe Owl is right. Maybe ghosts DON'T have birthdays!"

This was such a sad thought that Gabriel decided to go away for a while and forget all about birthdays. Nearby there was an old barn that looked as if it needed haunting. There went Gabriel.

But the barn was full of drafts at night and Gabriel grew homesick for Mr. and Mrs. Gould. His missed his friend, Owl, like anything. Sadly, Gabriel crossed off the last day of October. "Home I shall go," decided Gabriel, "birthday or not."

"Yoo-hoo!" hooted a voice.

Gabriel flew to a window.

"Nice smells in the kitchen!" whispered Owl. "Paper swishing in the dining room! Children whispering all over town!"

"IT'S MY BIRTHDAY!" shouted Gabriel, heading for home.

At first, he thought he couldn't believe his eyes. Then he decided that he could. There were shining candles and orange-and-black streamers and frosty cakes and dishes of ice cream! There were jolly jack-o'-lanterns at the windows and little bumpy presents at every plate! There were Mr. and Mrs. Gould, glowing like the candles on a cake! And, best of all, there were the girls and boys, as full of fun as a grab bag is full of surprises! And they were all dressed up like witches or owls or cats, or just like Gabriel himself!

"HAPPY HALLOWEEN!" called everybody.

"My birthday," thought Gabriel proudly, "even has a special name!" And at that, he sat right down with everybody else. Before very long, Gabriel decided that this was the most splendid birthday party that ever had been in the house at the edge of town.

The moon set late that night. At last Mr. and Mrs. Gould were sound asleep in their beds, and all the boys and girls were sound asleep in THEIR beds. At last Gabriel was alone in his little tower with all his lovely presents. There was a chain for Gabriel to rattle, a new sheet for Gabriel to wear for best, a paper hat that was just for fun, a jack-o'-lantern filled with nuts, and ever so many more things left around for Gabriel.

Just as the sun came up, which is when all good ghosts go to bed, Gabriel pulled the covers up under his chin. "Good night, Owl," he called lovingly.

Softly, from the tree outside the window, Owl sang Gabriel a birthday song:

"Happy Birthday to you-oooooo,
Happy Birthday to you-oooooo,
Happy Birthday, dear Gabriel,
Happy Birthday to you-oooooo!"

THE WIDE-AWAKE
COON-IN-THE-MIDDLE

WINTER was coming. Five fat raccoons sat down to supper in front of their cozy fire. There were Clarence Coon and Clementine Coon and their three Little Coons who wanted to hear all about hibernating.

"Sleeping all winter?" chuckled Clarence Coon. "Why, there's nothing like it! When the leaves start to fall, you go hunting for a nice snug house way up in a hollow tree."

"Like this?" said the Biggest Little Coon, looking around him happily.

"And then," smiled Clementine Coon, "you eat and eat and eat!"

"Like this?" laughed the Littlest Little Coon, starting right in.

"Just like this!" said Clementine. And she heaped their plates high with the yummiest food that ever was.

Clarence Coon, who was extremely fond of his wife's cooking, ate till he was all stretched out. Clementine Coon ate till she declared she couldn't hold another crumb. The Biggest Little Coon ate till he got round and warm and sleepy. And the Littlest Little Coon started snoozing right during dessert!

But no matter how much the Coon-in-the-Middle ate, he was still as wide-awake as a rooster. He watched the big white snowflakes falling lazily just outside the window. He wondered how they would feel on his nose and his toes and his soft fur coat.

"Well, well," said Clarence Coon, looking at his watch. "Time to hibernate!"

Sleepily Clementine puffed up the pillows. Yawning, Clarence spread the comforters. And when those three Little Coons were shining clean, Papa and Mama Coon heard their prayers and tucked them in.

"Have a nice winter," they said lovingly. Then off they tiptoed to bed, did Clarence and Clementine Coon. Deep under the blankets they snuggled and happily closed their eyes.

It was quiet and warm and dark. In the blink of an eye, the Biggest Little Coon and the Littlest Little Coon were snoozing soundly. But the wide-awake Coon-in-the-Middle just lay wide awake and listened to the snow against the pane.

"I'm not one bit sleepy," he said.

Clementine staggered to the stove. "More-you-eat-more-you-sleep," she mumbled, stirring warm milk on the stove. Then, being so very sleepy, she drank it all herself. Back she went to bed.

"I'm still wide awake," said that bright little Coon-in-the-Middle.

Clarence opened one eye. "Tell-you-story," he muttered. "Once-'pon-time. . ."

"Once upon a time, what?" said the Coon-in-the-Middle, with his round black eyes as shining as coals in the fire.

". . . lived-happily-ever-after," said Clarence, snoring splendidly.

Everybody was sound asleep. They would

be sound asleep for weeks and months. There would be no one to talk to till spring. Very lonely and sad was that wide-awake Coon-in-the-Middle.

So out of bed he crept. As quiet as a dream he tiptoed out into the frosty night. Everything looked strange and white from the door high up in the tree. Below, the snow was deep and soft.

"I'm going to dive into it!" whispered the Little Coon to himself.

And he did! Then he shoveled little tunnels with his nose. Then he rolled in it.

"Almost as good as swimming," he said, as excited as he could be. He rolled farther and farther away from the little house in the hollow tree.

After a while he began to wish he had someone to roll with. It was so dark and so still and so shivery.

But right then the wide-awake Coon heard something coming. He thought of an Indian. He thought of a dragon. He thought of his cozy bed, and his brothers all safe and sound asleep. He turned around and started for the hollow tree.

But all the paths were covered with snow.

That cold Little Coon didn't know which way to go. So he covered his furry face with his paws, and waited.

"Why, it's the Coon-in-the-Middle," chuckled somebody. The somebody was Granny Coon, and under her arm was a coon-size picture book. "For wide-awake coons," laughed Granny.

Almost before he knew it, that cold, wet, lost Little Coon was back home, all curled up in Granny's soft lap.

On the first page was a picture of a coon, yawning. The wide-awake Coon began to blink his eyes.

"Any Indians?" he said, turning the page. And there were some Indians, yawning widely. The Coon-in-the-Middle yawned once or twice.

"What, no dragons?" he said. He turned the page. Dragons, sure enough. Yawning, every one of them!

"Count them," said Granny Coon softly.

"One ... two ... three ..." And before he reached "four," that wide-awake Coon was not wide awake any more. When Granny tucked him in, all cozy for the winter, he didn't even know it!

THE THANKS-GIVING BEAR

IT WAS Thanksgiving Day. Grouchy Bear sat before the fire in his cozy kitchen, rock-rock-rocking in his chair.

"Bother!" he growled. "Nobody loves me. And it's Thanksgiving. And I haven't a single friend or relation to come and spend the day with me."

Just then the cuckoo popped his head out

of the cuckoo clock and called, "Cuckoo! Cuckoo! Cuckoo!"

"Oh, fiddle!" said Grouchy Bear. "Time to look at the turkey."

He opened the oven door and peered in. Delicious smells came floating out and made Grouchy's mouth water. He poked sadly at the tremendous turkey.

"Fat and juicy. Tender as a T," he said. "And nobody to eat it but me." He closed the oven door with a bang. "Time to start the vegetables," he sighed.

But what fun it would be, if only he had somebody to help him celebrate. He could PRETEND that friends and relations were coming. PRETENDING them was better than nothing. He started in by cutting up a very huge squash.

"Big as a full moon," Grouchy Bear said loudly, pretending very hard.

Now Grouchy Bear knew a lot of things.

He knew that to MAKE a friend you have to BE a friend. And that was exactly what he had done, all last week. Not once had he been grouchy. Not a single growl had he growled.

One morning he had met Tabitha Fox, coming home from the store.

"Good morning, Tabitha." He bowed politely. "May I carry your bundles for you?" And he had, too, all the way to her front door.

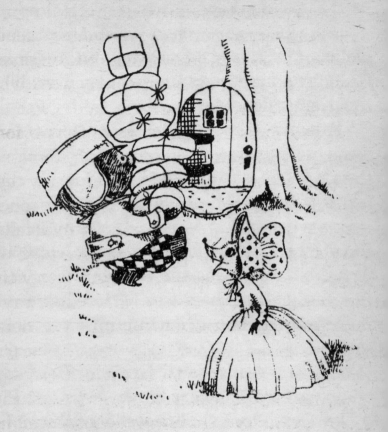

"How SPLENDID of you, Grouchy Bear!" she said.

That made Grouchy Bear feel so splendid that he whistled "Over the River and Through the Wood" all the way home.

But here it was Thanksgiving Day, and

he was as alone as a scarecrow. As alone as he had been last Thanksgiving and the Thanksgiving before that. It was enough to make anyone grouchy.

And yesterday, hadn't he been as friendly as anything to Gladys Goose? Gladys was shoveling the snow out of her path when Grouchy Bear came by.

"That," said Grouchy, "is not a job for a goose. Here, let me help you."

Gladys was delighted. Her beady eyes shone like currants in a pudding. "Grouchy Bear," she said, "we've all been mistaken. Why, you're real NEIGHBORLY!"

And Grouchy Bear felt so neighborly that he shoveled out Gladys Goose all the way to the road. And then—because being neighborly was such fun—he shoveled a neat path all the way to Gladys' woodpile.

In the afternoon he carried Hubert Pig's mail to him, and Elwell Skunk's to him, just to save them a trip to town. While at the post office, Grouchy Bear had even mailed off some picture post cards to his distant cousins, who lived on the other side of the woods.

But did he get in on anybody's Thanksgiving Day fun? Oh, no! Not he!

Grouchy Bear finished off the basket of potatoes. He started peeling a bushel of onions.

"I suppose," he told himself, "that Hubert Pig and Elwell Skunk are entertaining lots of friends and relations today."

By the time Grouchy Bear had put the last onion into the pot, the tears were streaming down his fat cheeks. "Bother these onions!" said Grouchy Bear. He mopped his eyes and he blew his nose. And he went back to his rocking chair and rocked very, very hard.

"Well, anyway," said Grouchy Bear, "I have a lot to be thankful for." He started counting his blessings on his fingers. "I'm thankful for my dinner that's cooking and filling my house with such lovely smells.

"I'm thankful for my cozy house," he continued. "And my comfy rocking chair. And the chances I have to be neighborly to all my friends and all the distant cousins."

By now, Grouchy Bear felt almost happy, he was so full of thanks.

Just then, the sleigh bells that hung on the door went JINGLE-INGLE-INGLE-INGLE! The door burst open and everybody was speaking at once.

"Happy Thanksgiving Day, Grouchy Bear!" called Tabitha Fox and Gladys Goose and Hubert Pig and Elwell Skunk and a number of the distant cousins from the other side of the wood.

Grouchy Bear's eyes shone like shiny chestnuts. He began to feel so full of happiness that his jacket grew very tight.

"We all felt..." began Tabitha Fox gaily.

"...that all of us nice friends and relations..." smiled Gladys Goose.

"...ought to be thankful we have one another!" cried Hubert Pig and Elwell Skunk, both together.

"So we decided to spend Thanksgiving Day with our favorite bear," chorused the distant cousins from the other side of the wood.

Grouchy Bear beamed all the way from one of his furry ears to the other. He was so full of happiness that his buttons came popping off his jacket, POP, POP, POP.

The cuckoo peeped out of the cuckoo clock and called "Cuckoo! Cuckoo! Cuckoo!"

"Time for all good friends and relations to sit down at the table," cried Grouchy Bear happily. "Time to give thanks."

And they did, every one of them!

GIANT GRUMBY'S
CHRISTMAS

ONCE there was a giant who lived in a castle on the top of a hill. His name was Giant Grumby, and he was as big and as cross a giant as you could hope to see.

One day Giant Grumby was sitting all alone in his castle, counting his gold. "One million and one, one million and two..."

Right then he happened to look down

toward the village at the foot of the hill and he saw all sorts of things happening. He saw wreaths being hung in doorways, and candles being placed in windows. He saw people with packages, and children running around with their faces lighted up like Christmas trees.

Giant Grumby hurried to his calendar and ran his finger along the dates. "Oh, no!" groaned Giant Grumby. "NOT Christmas again! NOT deck the hall, and ring the bells, and fa-la-la-la-la! Stuff and nonsense!"

Back he stumped to his gold. "One million and . . ." But Giant Grumby had lost count. "Christmas," he said, suddenly remembering the shiny red sled he had always wanted, and the peppermint-striped stocking cap and mittens. "Christmas?" said Giant Grumby, and he nodded to himself. Why not have himself the best Christmas ever—the shiny red sled, the peppermint-striped cap and mittens?

Down to the village marched Giant Grumby. As he went, the thought of a Christmas for himself was such a wonderfully happy thought that his stomach turned a big somersault. "FA-LA-LA-LA-LA," sang Giant Grumby. He sang so loudly that everybody stopped right in the middle of Christmas shopping, and ran home and hid under the bed—everybody except the shopkeeper.

"Merry Christmas!" said the shopkeeper.

"Merry Christmas?" asked Giant Grumby. "Merry Christmas to me?"

"A VERY Merry Christmas!" smiled the shopkeeper.

Giant Grumby thought a minute. "The same to you," he said. "And I want to buy a shiny red sled, my size—and a peppermint-striped cap and mittens, my size."

"Oh dear, dear, dear," said the shopkeeper. "Sleds your size are hardest to get. Caps and mittens your size are just what we don't have."

"Posh and bother!" said Giant Grumby. "Then give me all the toys in the store!" And he dumped a big bag of gold upside down on the counter.

"But they're not your size," said the shopkeeper.

"STUFF AND NONSENSE!" said Giant Grumby in a giant voice.

"Yes, sir," said the shopkeeper. "Right away, sir."

Soon the giant was piled high with packages and he went stamping off up the hill.

Then everybody came out from under their beds. They asked the shopkeeper what Giant Grumby wanted.

"He wanted a sled," said the shopkeeper sadly, "his size. And a stocking cap and mittens. His hands and ears looked cold."

"Oh, poor Giant Grumby!" said all the children, very much troubled. The thought of anybody not getting a thing he wanted on Christmas was a sad thought for Christmas Eve.

"I have an idea!" said the shopkeeper's boy. He whispered his idea to the shopkeeper.

"Yes, we have wood," nodded the shopkeeper. "And wool, too, and knitting needles." Everybody's face lighted up exactly like a Christmas tree—just the way Giant Grumby's face was NOT lighted up!

Into his lonely castle went Giant Grumby. He dumped the toys in the middle of the floor and poked among them sadly. He could just squeeze his little toe onto the roller skates. As for the bicycles, he couldn't fit on one! Everything was much too small for a giant.

"Just as I thought," sighed Giant Grumby, blinking back a tear. Then he sat down and ate a lonely supper of pickle sandwiches.

"Christmas must be nice," thought Giant Grumby, "for some people." He thought so long and so hard about the nice kind of Christmas that before he knew it his eyes had closed. He was sound asleep.

"Now!" whispered the shopkeeper's boy.

Into the castle tiptoed the children. Very softly, so as not to wake him, they laid something beside Giant Grumby. Then, down through the frosty night, they ran home to bed, as quiet as snowflakes.

Very early Christmas morning, Giant Grumby woke up. He rubbed his eyes and stared at what was on the floor beside him. "A shiny red sled," whispered Giant Grumby, "just my size! And a peppermint-striped cap and a pair of mittens, just my size!" And tied to the sled was a big red bow with a card that said MERRY CHRISTMAS TO GIANT GRUMBY.

Giant Grumby just smiled and smiled. Then he looked at the big pile of toys in the middle of the floor. "Just their size," nodded Giant Grumby. "And there's still time before they wake up!"

Then Giant Grumby pulled on his peppermint-striped stocking cap and his beautiful new mittens. He piled the toys onto his brand-new red sled. Then off down the snowy hill he coasted.

"Fa-la-la-la-la," sang Giant Grumby. He sang very softly, so as not to wake up a single child that wonderful morning!

THE SLEEPYHEAD
COON-IN-THE-MIDDLE

CLARENCE COON opened one sleepy eye. Then he opened both eyes and looked at the clock and became as wide-awake as a robin.

"IT'S SPRING!" he shouted. "QUARTER-PAST SPRING," he said, bounding out of bed. "EVERYBODY UP!"

Clementine Coon smiled fondly at her husband. "Goodness me," said she, "I've been up for three days already!"

Clarence gave her a big coon-size hug. He looked hungrily over her shoulder. "Looks like quite a breakfast."

"A picnic breakfast," nodded Clementine. "When folks have slept all winter long, what they need is a GREAT BIG PICNIC BREAKFAST." At that, the Biggest Little Coon woke up and yawned. The Littlest Little Coon woke up and stretched. But the sleepyhead Coon-in-the-Middle just kept right on snoozing.

Out of bed rolled the two wide-awake Little Coons, thinking how hungry they were. They were bigger than when they went to bed, back in the fall. And they were ten times emptier!

"Is hibernating over?" asked the Biggest little Coon.

"Hibernating's over," smiled Clementine Coon, hugging her two hungry coons.

"Is it time to eat?" asked the Littlest Little Coon.

"Time to eat," chuckled Clarence. And he tossed into the air first one bright-eyed Little Coon, and then the other.

"Up with the sleepyhead Coon-in-the-Middle!" he shouted cheerfully. He seized a pan and banged on it as everyone sang:

Clickity, clackity, clumpity, clum,
Winter's over, sleeping's done.
Time for food and time for fun!

But the sleepyhead Coon-in-the-Middle kept right on snoozing!

"Let's let him sleep till Tuesday," smiled Clementine Coon lovingly. But they left a note on the table, just in case.

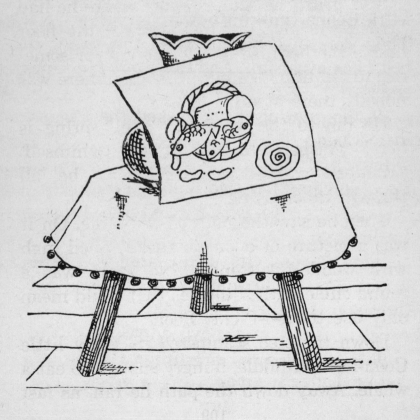

Then off they tiptoed, all those wide-awake, bright-awake coons. Down the tree they slipped, as quiet as shadows. Away they went to Picnic Pool, with their picnic breakfast.

And the sleepyhead Coon-in-the-Middle kept right on sleeping. He dreamed he was sliding down Sliding Rock right into Picnic Pool. He landed in the water with a loud CRASH! And right then he was wide awake.

"Oh, dear," he said, rubbing where he had landed. He picked himself up off the floor beside the bed. He looked around for someone to tell him it didn't hurt—but there was nobody there at all!

He ran to the window. "Why, spring is here!" whispered that Little Coon to himself. "Winter's over. Everybody must be all through hibernating."

Then he saw the note on the table. On it was a picture of a picnic basket piled high with wonderful things. And there was a round circle with squiggles that could mean only one thing—Picnic Pool!

Down the tree scampered that gay little Coon-in-the-Middle, hungry enough to eat a whale. Away down the path he ran, as fast as his furry legs could carry him. And as he ran, he thought some splendid thoughts. He thought of fish fried in butter. And turtle eggs done to a T. And berries basted with honey. And melons, juicy and sweet.

He stopped to sniff at a nice skunk cabbage. And that is when he heard the Big Noise, crashing along the path! The Little Coon-in-the-Middle thought how alone he was in the big dark wood. Under the skunk cabbage he crept. And there he waited with his heart going POM-POM-POM.

The Big Noise came right up to the skunk cabbage—and stopped. His heart went POM-POM-POM, faster and louder than ever. Then in Granny Coon's nice chuckly voice, the Big Noise said, "Well, if it isn't the Coon-in-the-Middle! I thought you were sound asleep."

Out popped the Coon-in-the-Middle, his eyes as shiny as berries. "Nope, I'm wide awake," he told her. "And I'm as hungry as ten bears!"

"So am I!" laughed Granny Coon.

And on to the Picnic Pool ran Granny Coon and that wide-awake Coon-in-the-Middle. Side by side they ran, as hungry as *twenty* bears!

A HAT FOR CRUMPET

CRUMPET was a big friendly trolley-horse. "Maybe I shouldn't say so," declared Crumpet. "But I suppose I'm the biggest, friendliest trolley-horse in all New York!"

Crumpet was right. Wherever she went, CLIPPITY-CLOP, East Side, West Side, all around the town, people looked twice at Crumpet. Even the Mayor.

"And I suppose," thought Crumpet happily, "that Billy Bailey is the snappiest-looking driver anywhere at all."

Sure enough. Bill Bailey sat high and handsome on the driver's seat behind Crumpet. He tipped his hat to everyone as snappily as you please.

"Without a doubt," went on Crumpet, looking over her shoulder, "our trolley is the prettiest little trolley you ever did see."

And it was, indeed. Golden squiggles all over the sides. Scallops on the top. "And the nicest people in New York," Crumpet decided, "sitting on the red plush seats." The mothers in their neat straw hats. The fathers in their derbies. The dearest and the cleanest children in the world. And ONE fine spring morning, the Mayor himself!

"Top of the morning, Bill Bailey!" he boomed. "And what's an elegant horse like Crumpet doing without a hat? Every trolley-horse in New York has a hat!"

Elegant! The Mayor called her ELEGANT! Pointing her toes, Crumpet trotted off so smartly that all the nice passengers held onto their hats to keep from losing them.

"Sure, Your Honor," laughed Bill Bailey. "I'll get her a hat for Easter."

All the way down Fifth Avenue Crumpet peered into the hat shops. She wondered which hat Bill Bailey would buy. "Maybe," she thought, "it will be that sailor hat with the ribbons down the back. Or maybe," whispered Crumpet, "one of those wide, beautiful, ELEGANT hats with roses around the brim!" At the very thought, Crumpet did a two-step all the way to City Hall.

That night Crumpet dreamed about hats —all sorts of hats. And every one of them was beautiful and fancy.

Next morning, in came Bill Bailey with Crumpet's breakfast. And something else.

"Here you are, Crumpet!" he sang. "Here's the comfiest, droopiest old hat anywhere in town! Found it on the dump!" And Bill Bailey, because he loved Crumpet, carefully cut two large holes for Crumpet's ears. He put the hat on Crumpet's head. "Very snappy!" said Bill Bailey. Then off they started up the Avenue.

Poor Crumpet. Maybe, if she tiptoed very softly . . . and hung her head very low . . . maybe nobody would notice . . .

"WHAT'S THE MATTER WITH CRUMPET?" everybody asked.

"I wish I knew," worried Bill Bailey.

"I hate to say it," said the Mayor, "but an elegant trolley like this trolley needs an elegant horse to pull it."

All the nice passengers stared at Crumpet, dragging her feet up ahead. "What's the matter with Crumpet?" they asked one another.

But the children, who loved Crumpet very much, knew exactly what was the matter. They whispered to Bill Bailey. Bill Bailey said, "Well, what do you know!" Then, "Maybe you're right!" And finally, "A splendid idea!!!"

Crumpet, with her head hanging down by her knees and the old hat drooping over her eyes, heard the whispers. Then she heard the secret clinking of many pennies and dimes. Then, right in front of a hat shop, she

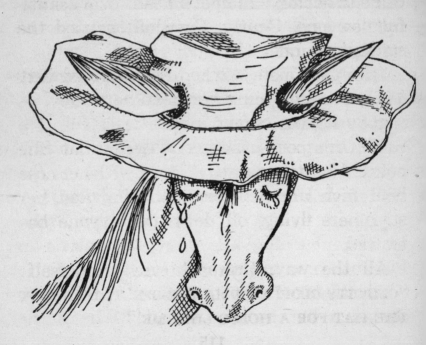

heard the CLANG-CLANG of the trolley-bell. Crumpet stopped. Passengers got off. Crumpet's heart was so heavy that she didn't even wonder what Bill Bailey was waiting for. She squeezed her eyes tight shut to hold back the big tears.

Then a voice said softly, "Crumpet, this is for you."

Crumpet lifted her head. There beside her were the children, taking something out of a box. A something that was wide and beautiful and elegant! It was blooming with roses and streaming with streamers! Off came the comfy old hat. On went the beautiful new one. Gently, the children tied the streamers under Crumpet's chin.

"Happy Easter, Crumpet!" they smiled. Then they hopped back onto the trolley.

CLANG-CLANG-CLANG! went the bell. Up came Crumpet's head in the elegant hat. She pointed her toes daintily. Then, with her nose held high and her roses bobbing and her streamers flying, off down the avenue she trotted.

All the way, Crumpet sang to herself: "CLIPPITY-CLOP! TWIDDLE-DEE-DEE! THIS IS JUST THE HAT FOR A HORSE LIKE ME!"

LITTLE BEAR AND
THE BEE TREE

Way down deep in the green forest there was a little grove of white birch trees. Deep inside this grove was a little black cave.

Deep inside this little black cave was a little brown bear.

And deep inside this little brown bear was a little golden honey.

The little brown bear did not think that a little golden honey was enough golden honey. He decided to go and hunt for more. Softly he walked out of the little black cave, and out of the little grove of white birch trees. Very s-o-o-oftly he walked through the green forest and down a quiet path which turned and became another quiet path which turned and became another quiet path which turned and became another quiet path.

BZZZZZZZZ-ZZ-ZZ-ZZ-ZZ-ZZ-ZZ-ZZ-ZZ-ZZ!!

There, ahead of him in the green forest, was a sunny little clearing. In the sunny little clearing was an old brown bee tree. And in the old brown bee tree was lots and lots of golden honey, and LOTS and LOTS of buzz-z-z-zing bees.

The little brown bear looked at the old brown bee tree and wondered. He wondered how he could get some of that golden honey out of the brown bee tree without being stung by the buzzing bees.

So he sat down, quietly, to wonder.

Suddenly the clearing was filled with noise. BZZ-ZZ-ZZ-ZZ! That was the first noise. GRR-R-R! O-O-O-O-O-O-O-O-OW! That was the next noise.

Can you guess what happened? That little brown bear, while looking at the tree, had sat down exactly on a honeybee! The bee had stung the little bear—hard!

And that wasn't all. The little brown bear jumped off that bee so fast that he landed right in the middle of the old bee tree.

He closed his eyes and waited.

But do you know, when those bees saw the GIANT bear sailing toward them through the air, they took off in a lo-o-o-o-o-ong line that hummed like a plucked banjo string. Straight out of the clearing and into the forest they hummed.

They never came back, not ever.

And the little brown bear? Well, way down deep in the green forest is the sunny little clearing. And deep inside the sunny little clearing is the old brown bee tree. And deep inside the old brown bee tree is—you guessed it!—the little brown bear. And deep inside the little brown bear is lots and lots and LOTS and LOTS of golden honey!

GRANNY BLAKE AND

HER WONDERFUL CAKE

ONCE there was an old woman who baked good cakes to sell. From morning till night her little house was filled with wonderful smells. Chocolate cake and lemon cake and peppermint cake and plum cake. Angel cake and devil's cake and cinnamon cake and cheesecake. Any kind of cake a body could name, Granny Blake could bake.

All over town, the mothers and fathers

ordered cakes from Granny Blake. Birthday cakes for the girls and boys. Welcome cakes for the new neighbors. Wedding cakes for the brides. Even a thank-you cake for the town band. Granny Blake made them all. She never once said no to a single soul.

"Not I," said Granny Blake. "Any cake you want, I'll bake. For I like folks and folks like cake."

Now, with all these orders coming in, you might think that Granny Blake would see lots of folks and eat lots of cake. But no, indeed. What with the measuring and the mixing and the beating and the baking, Granny Blake never had a minute nor a crumb to herself. Not even just before her own birthday, which she didn't once think of.

"Take a day off," said the mothers and fathers when they came for their cakes. "Get someone in to help."

But Granny Blake smiled and shook her head. "Everyone is too busy," she said. And she went right on with her measuring and her mixing.

"Take a week off," said the children when they came to clean out the bowls. "Tell people No."

But Granny Blake just shook her head. "You'll not hear No from Granny Blake, for I like folks and folks like cake." And she went right on with her beating and her baking.

"This is a fine how-do-you-do!" everybody said. "Too busy to remember her own birthday! Too busy, even to make herself a cake!"

All over town they started to whisper. "Do you suppose?" And "Why not?" And finally, "Let's do it!"

"Can you bake us a cake," they said to Granny Blake, "BIG ENOUGH FOR THE WHOLE TOWN?"

"Well, I just will," smiled Granny Blake, who never said No to a single soul. "Only how can I ever measure such a great cake? And how shall I ever mix it and beat it and bake it? And wherever shall I put it when it is done? I declare. I do not know!"

But everybody else knew. Because—first, the boys and girls came running with their biggest sand pails to help with all the measuring. Next, the new neighbors brought a big cement mixer to help with all the mixing and the beating. After that, to help with the baking, each bride popped a different panful of batter into her own oven. Pretty soon the good smells started rising all over town. Chocolate, lemon, peppermint, plum—several of each kind—to please everybody.

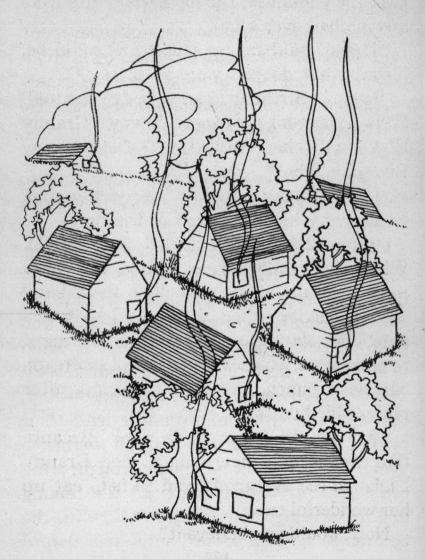

As soon as the cakes were baked, the town band fitted them all together on the bandstand, right in the middle of the park. And, last of all, Granny Blake frosted it—the biggest, the yummiest, the most wonderful cake anyone had ever seen!

"There!" said she, as pleased as could be. "Now, what do you want it to say?"

"Happy Birthday," everybody shouted.

"H-A-P-P-Y B-I-R-T-H-D-A-Y," wrote Granny Blake with her decorating tube. "Happy Birthday, who?"

"Happy Birthday to YOU!" everybody sang. "And many happy returns of the day!"

Granny Blake just smiled and smiled. When the candles were lighted, she blew them out, all in one puff. The town band started playing when she opened her presents. They played right through the serving of refreshments, which were gallons of ice cream, barrels of punch, and of course, plate after plate of birthday cake.

They played for a whole week. Because that was exactly how long it took Granny Blake to see everybody and to help eat up her wonderful cake.

Now, would you believe it?

THE LITTLE LOST CAT
AND THE VERY
SMALL WITCH

A LITTLE lost cat tiptoed through the woods. Then he stopped to listen. The night was very big and still.

124

The night wind whispered "Sh-sh-sh-sh."

Way up high in the sky, the moon blinked behind a cloud, like a great cat's eye. The little cat winked back.

"Maybe tonight I'll find a home," he said. "Something to eat, and someone to love me. Maybe tonight."

Down through the cold and magic night he trotted, looking and looking.

Suddenly he stopped. In a clearing ahead burned a bonfire, bright and warm. Its yellow light danced round and round, so that the clearing was like a bright little room in the deep woods.

The little lost cat sniffed the air. He smelled the pine boughs crackling in the fire. He smelled the rich stew bubbling in the big iron pot.

"Something to eat," he said.

The little cat crept closer. He saw—a witch! Such a very small witch, crying all alone into her pinafore.

"Someone to love," said the little cat, hopefully.

He rubbed, purring, against the round legs of the very small witch.

Surprised, the little witch looked down.

"A cat," she said. "Oh, it must be a little lost cat."

She picked up the little cat and held him snug and warm in her arms.

"Now I can go, too," she said, drying her eyes.

"Go where?" said the little cat sadly.

"Up in the sky like The Others. Up in the sky with you," whispered the very small witch. "There were not enough cats for me to have one. And no witch can ride her broomstick without a cat. Don't you know what night this is?"

"Wednesday," said the little cat.

"It's something else, too." The very small witch placed her mouth close to the little cat's fuzzy ear. "It's—Halloween," she whispered.

"Oh," said the little cat. A shiver like a baby wind ran along his furry back. A happy sort of shiver.

"Come," said the very small witch. "There is no time to lose."

She set out a dish of stew for the little cat. The stew tasted rich and warm and yummy and the dish was just the right size.

Then the little witch smoothed out her

126

pinafore, and washed her face with dew. She fastened around her shoulders a much-too-big black cloak. She put on her head a tall peaked hat that came down over her ears. But she looked beautiful to the little cat.

Then she mounted her tiny broomstick. The little cat jumped behind her onto the sweet straw.

For a moment they waited in that big, still, magic night. Then, from somewhere above, came the happy howling of a witch's cat. The little cat felt the broomstick rise into the great night sky. He looked down. Below lay the dark woods, with the bonfire still gleaming like a tiny star. Ahead glowed the moon like a great cat's eye.

The little cat's stomach was full and warm. He had found something to eat.

In front of him rode the very small witch, as happy as could be. He had found someone to love.

The little cat turned round and round in the sweet straw. He tucked his nose into the folds of the long black cloak of the very small witch.

Then, because he was not lost any more, he fell sound asleep up near the magic moon.

Use this easy, convenient way to build your child's library of
Read-Aloud Books